'Ah, life of a human being – a drop of dew, a flash of lightning? This is so sad, so sad.'

RYŪNOSUKE AKUTAGAWA
Born 1892, Tokyo
Died 1927, Tokyo

This selection is taken from Jay Rubin's translation of
Rashōmon and Seventeen Other Stories, first published in 2006.

RYŪNOSUKE AKUTAGAWA IN PENGUIN CLASSICS
Rashōmon and Seventeen Other Stories

RYŪNOSUKE AKUTAGAWA

The Life of a Stupid Man

Translated by
Jay Rubin

PENGUIN BOOKS

PENGUIN CLASSICS

UK | USA | Canada | Ireland | Australia
India | New Zealand | South Africa

Penguin Books is part of the Penguin Random House group of companies
whose addresses can be found at global.penguinrandomhouse.com.

This selection published in Penguin Classics 2015

027

Translation copyright © Jay Rubin, 2006

The moral right of the translator has been asserted

Set in 9.5/13 pt Baskerville 10 Pro
Typeset by Jouve (UK), Milton Keynes
Printed in Great Britain by Clays Ltd, Elcograf S.p.A.

A CIP catalogue record for this book is available from the British Library

ISBN: 978-0-141-39772-6

www.greenpenguin.co.uk

Contents

In a Bamboo Grove

THE TESTIMONY OF A WOODCUTTER
UNDER QUESTIONING BY THE MAGISTRATE

That is true, Your Honor. I am the one who found the body. I went out as usual this morning to cut cedar in the hills behind my place. The body was in a bamboo grove on the other side of the mountain. Its exact location? A few hundred yards off the Yamashina post road. A deserted place where a few scrub cedar trees are mixed in with the bamboo.

The man was lying on his back in his pale blue robe with the sleeves tied up and one of those fancy Kyoto-style black hats with the sharp creases. He had only one stab wound, but it was right in the middle of his chest; the bamboo leaves around the body were soaked with dark red blood. No, the bleeding had stopped. The wound looked dry, and I remember it had a big horsefly sucking on it so hard the thing didn't even notice my footsteps.

Did I see a sword or anything? No, Sir, not a thing. Just a length of rope by the cedar tree next to the body.

And – oh yes, there was a comb there, too. Just the rope and the comb is all. But the weeds and the bamboo leaves on the ground were pretty trampled down: he must have put up a tremendous fight before they killed him. How's that, Sir – a horse? No, a horse could never have gotten into that place. It's all bamboo thicket between there and the road.

THE TESTIMONY OF A TRAVELING PRIEST UNDER QUESTIONING BY THE MAGISTRATE

I'm sure I passed the man yesterday, Your Honor. Yesterday at – about noon, I'd say. Near Checkpoint Hill on the way to Yamashina. He was walking toward the checkpoint with a woman on horseback. She wore a stiff, round straw hat with a long veil hanging down around the brim; I couldn't see her face, just her robe. I think it had a kind of dark-red outer layer with a blue-green lining. The horse was a dappled gray with a tinge of red, and I'm fairly sure it had a clipped mane. Was it a big horse? I'd say it was a few inches taller than most, but I'm a priest after all. I don't know much about horses. The man? No, Sir, he had a good-sized sword, and he was equipped with a bow and arrows. I can still see that black-lacquered quiver of his: he must have had twenty arrows in it, maybe more. I would never have dreamt that a thing like this could happen to such a man. Ah, what is the life of a human being – a drop of dew, a flash of lightning? This is so sad, so sad. What can I say?

THE TESTIMONY OF A POLICEMAN UNDER QUESTIONING BY THE MAGISTRATE

The man I captured, Your Honor? I am certain he is the famous bandit, Tajōmaru. True, when I caught him he had fallen off his horse, and he was moaning and groaning on the stone bridge at Awataguchi. The time, Sir? It was last night at the first watch. He was wearing the same dark blue robe and carrying the same long sword he used the time I almost captured him before. You can see he also has a bow and arrows now. Oh, is that so, Sir? The dead man, too? That settles it, then: I'm sure this Tajōmaru fellow is the murderer. A leather-wrapped bow, a quiver in black lacquer, seventeen hawk-feather arrows – they must have belonged to the victim. And yes, as you say, Sir, the horse is a dappled gray with a touch of red, and it has a clipped mane. It's only a dumb animal, but it gave that bandit just what he deserved, throwing him like that. It was a short way beyond the bridge, trailing its reins on the ground and eating plume grass by the road.

Of all the bandits prowling around Kyoto, this Tajōmaru is known as a fellow who likes the women. Last fall, people at Toribe Temple found a pair of worshippers murdered – a woman and a child – on the hill behind the statue of Binzuru. Everybody said Tajōmaru must have done it. If it turns out he killed the man, there's no telling what he might have done to the woman who was on the horse. I don't mean to meddle, Sir, but I do think you ought to question him about that.

THE TESTIMONY OF AN OLD WOMAN UNDER QUESTIONING BY THE MAGISTRATE

Yes, Your Honor, my daughter was married to the dead man. He is not from the capital, though. He was a samurai serving in the Wakasa provincial office. His name was Kanazawa no Takehiro, and he was twenty-six years old. No, Sir, he was a very kind man. I can't believe anyone would have hated him enough to do this.

My daughter, Sir? Her name is Masago, and she is nineteen years old. She's as bold as any man, but the only man she has ever known is Takehiro. Her complexion is a little on the dark side, and she has a mole by the outside corner of her left eye, but her face is a tiny, perfect oval.

Takehiro left for Wakasa yesterday with my daughter, but what turn of fate could have led to this? There's nothing I can do for my son-in-law anymore, but what could have happened to my daughter? I'm worried sick about her. Oh please, Sir, do everything you can to find her, leave no stone unturned: I have lived a long time, but I have never wanted anything so badly in my life. Oh how I hate that bandit – that, that Tajōmaru! Not only my son-in-law, but my daughter . . . (Here the old woman broke down and was unable to go on speaking.)

*   *   *   *   *

TAJŌMARU'S CONFESSION

Sure, I killed the man. But I didn't kill the woman. So, where did she go? I don't know any better than you do. Now, wait just a minute – you can torture me all you want, but I can't tell you what I don't know. And besides, now that you've got me, I'm not going to hide anything. I'm no coward.

I met that couple yesterday, a little after noon. The second I saw them, a puff of wind lifted her veil and I caught a peek at her. Just a peek: that's maybe why she looked so perfect to me – an absolute bodhisattva of a woman. I made up my mind right then to take her even if I had to kill the man.

Oh come on, killing a man is not as big a thing as people like you seem to think. If you're going to take somebody's woman, a man has to die. When *I* kill a man, I do it with my sword, but people like you don't use swords. You gentlemen kill with your power, with your money, and sometimes just with your words: you tell people you're doing them a favor. True, no blood flows,

5

the man is still alive, but you've killed him all the same. I don't know whose sin is greater – yours or mine. (A sarcastic smile.)

Of course, if you can take the woman without killing the man, all the better. Which is exactly what I was hoping to do yesterday. It would have been impossible on the Yamashina post road, of course, so I thought of a way to lure them into the hills.

It was easy. I fell in with them on the road and made up a story. I told them I had found an old burial mound in the hills, and when I opened it it was full of swords and mirrors and things. I said I had buried the stuff in a bamboo grove on the other side of the mountain to keep anyone from finding out about it, and I'd sell it cheap to the right buyer. He started getting interested soon enough. It's scary what greed can do to people, don't you think? In less than an hour, I was leading that couple and their horse up a mountain trail.

When we reached the grove, I told them the treasure was buried in there and they should come inside with me and look at it. The man was so hungry for the stuff by then, he couldn't refuse, but the woman said she'd wait there on the horse. I figured that would happen – the woods are so thick. They fell right into my trap. We left the woman alone and went into the grove.

It was all bamboo at first. Fifty yards or so inside, there was a sort of open clump of cedars – the perfect place for what I was going to do. I pushed through the thicket and made up some nonsense about how the treasure was buried under one of them. When he heard that, the man charged toward some scrawny cedars visible up ahead. The bamboo thinned out, and the trees were standing there in a row. As soon as we got to them, I grabbed him and pinned him down. I could see he was a strong man – he carried a sword – but I took him by surprise, and he couldn't do a thing. I had him tied to the base of a tree in no time. Where did I get the rope? Well, I'm a thief, you know – I might have to scale a wall at any time – so I've always got a piece of rope in my belt. I stuffed his mouth full of bamboo leaves to keep him quiet. That's all there was to it.

Once I finished with the man, I went and told the woman that her husband had suddenly been taken ill and she should come and have a look at him. This was another bull's-eye, of course. She took off her hat and let me lead her by the hand into the grove. As soon as she saw the man tied to the tree, though, she whipped a dagger out of her breast. I never saw a woman with such fire! If I'd been off my guard, she'd have stuck that thing in my gut. And the way she kept coming, she would have done me some damage eventually no matter how much I dodged. Still, I *am* Tajōmaru. One way or another, I managed to knock the knife out of her hand without drawing my sword. Even the most spirited woman is going to be helpless if she hasn't got a weapon. And so I was able to make the woman mine without taking her husband's life.

Yes, you heard me: without taking her husband's life. I wasn't planning to kill him on top of everything else. The woman was on the ground, crying, and I was getting ready to run out of the grove and leave her there when all of a sudden she grabbed my arm like some kind of crazy person. And then I heard what she was shouting between sobs. She could hardly catch her breath: 'Either you die or my husband dies. It has to be one of you. It's worse than death for me to have two men see my shame. I want to stay with the one left alive, whether it's you or him.' That gave me a wild desire to kill her husband. (Sullen excitement.)

When I say this, you probably think I'm crueler than you are. But that's because you didn't see the look on her face – and especially, you never saw the way her eyes were burning at that moment. When those eyes met mine, I knew I wanted to make her my wife. Let the thunder god kill me, I'd make her my wife – that was the only thought in my head. And no, not just from lust. I know that's what you gentlemen are thinking. If lust was all I felt for her, I'd already taken care of that. I could've just kicked her down and gotten out of there. And the man wouldn't have stained my sword with his blood. But the moment my eyes locked onto hers in that dark grove, I knew I couldn't leave there until I had killed him.

Still, I didn't want to kill him in a cowardly way. I untied him and challenged him to a sword fight. (That piece of rope they found was the one I threw aside then.) The man looked furious as he drew his big sword, and without a word he sprang at me in a rage. I don't have to tell you the outcome of the fight. My sword pierced his breast on the twenty-third thrust. Not till the twenty-third: I want you to keep that in mind. I still admire him for that. He's the only man who ever lasted even twenty thrusts with me. (Cheerful grin.)

As he went down, I lowered my bloody sword and turned toward the woman. But she was gone! I looked for her among the cedars, but the bamboo leaves on the ground showed no sign she'd ever been there. I cocked my ear for any sound of her, but all I could hear was the man's death rattle.

Maybe she had run through the underbrush to call for help when the sword fight started. The thought made me fear for my life. I grabbed the man's sword and his bow and arrows and headed straight for the mountain road. The woman's horse was still there, just chewing on grass. Anything else I could tell you after that would be a waste of breath. I got rid of his sword before coming to Kyoto, though.

So that's my confession. I always knew my head would end up hanging in the tree outside the prison some day, so let me have the ultimate punishment. (Defiant attitude.)

9

Ryūnosuke Akutagawa

PENITENT CONFESSION OF A
WOMAN IN THE KIYOMIZU TEMPLE

After the man in the dark blue robe had his way with me, he looked at my husband, all tied up, and taunted him with laughter. How humiliated my husband must have felt! He squirmed and twisted in the ropes that covered his body, but the knots ate all the deeper into his flesh. Stumbling, I ran to his side. No – I *tried* to run to him, but instantly the man kicked me down. And that was when it happened: that was when I saw the indescribable glint in my husband's eyes. Truly, it was indescribable. It makes me shudder to recall it even now. My husband was unable to speak a word, and yet, in that moment, his eyes conveyed his whole heart to me. What I saw shining there was neither anger nor sorrow. It was the cold flash of contempt – contempt for *me*. This struck me more painfully than the bandit's kick. I let out a cry and collapsed on the spot.

When I regained consciousness, the man in blue was gone. The only one there in the grove was my husband, still tied to the cedar tree. I just barely managed to raise myself on the carpet of dead bamboo leaves, and look into my husband's face. His eyes were exactly as they had been before, with that same cold look of contempt and hatred. How can I describe the emotion that filled my heart then? Shame . . . sorrow . . . anger . . . I staggered over to him.

'Oh, my husband! Now that this has happened, I

cannot go on living with you. I am prepared to die here and now. But you – yes, I want you to die as well. You witnessed my shame. I cannot leave you behind with that knowledge.'

I struggled to say everything I needed to say, but my husband simply went on staring at me in disgust. I felt as if my breast would burst open at any moment, but holding my feelings in check, I began to search the bamboo thicket for his sword. The bandit must have taken it – I couldn't find it anywhere – and my husband's bow and arrows were gone as well. But then I had the good luck to find the dagger at my feet. I brandished it before my husband and spoke to him once again.

'This is the end, then. Please be so good as to allow me to take your life. I will quickly follow you in death.'

When he heard this, my husband finally began moving his lips. Of course his mouth was stuffed with bamboo leaves, so he couldn't make a sound, but I knew immediately what he was saying. With total contempt for me, he said only, 'Do it.' Drifting somewhere between dream and reality, I thrust the dagger through the chest of his pale blue robe.

Then I lost consciousness again. When I was able to look around me at last, my husband, still tied to the tree, was no longer breathing. Across his ashen face shone a streak of light from the setting sun, filtered through the bamboo and cedar. Gulping back my tears, I untied him and cast the rope aside. And then – and then what happened to me? I no longer have the strength to tell it. That I failed to kill myself is obvious. I tried to stab myself in the throat. I threw myself in a pond at the foot of the mountain. Nothing worked. I am still here, by no means proud of my inability to die. (Forlorn smile.) Perhaps even Kanzeon, bodhisattva of compassion, has turned away from me for being so weak. But now – now that I have killed my husband, now that I have been violated by a bandit – what am I to do? Tell me, what am I to . . . (Sudden violent sobbing.)

THE TESTIMONY OF THE DEAD MAN'S SPIRIT TOLD THROUGH A MEDIUM

After the bandit had his way with my wife, he sat there on the ground, trying to comfort her. I could say nothing, of course, and I was bound to the cedar tree. But I kept trying to signal her with my eyes: *Don't believe anything he tells you. He's lying, no matter what he says.* I tried to convey my meaning to her, but she just went on cringing there on the fallen bamboo leaves, staring at her knees. And, you know, I could see she was listening to him. I writhed with jealousy, but the bandit kept his smooth talk going from one point to the next. 'Now that your flesh has been sullied, things will never be the same with your husband. Don't stay with him – come and be my wife! It's because

I love you so much that I was so wild with you.' The bandit had the gall to speak to her like that!

When my wife raised her face in response to him, she seemed almost spellbound. I had never seen her look so beautiful as she did at that moment. And what do you think this beautiful wife of mine said to the bandit, in my presence – in the presence of her husband bound hand and foot? My spirit may be wandering now between one life and the next, but every time I recall her answer, I burn with indignation. 'All right,' she told him, 'take me any-where you like.' (Long silence.)

And that was not her only crime against me. If that were all she did, I would not be suffering so here in the darkness. With him leading her by the hand, she was stepping out of the bamboo grove as if in a dream, when suddenly the color drained from her face and she pointed back to me. 'Kill him!' she screamed. 'Kill him! I can't be with you as long as he is alive!' Again and again she screamed, as if she had lost her mind, 'Kill him!' Even now her words like a windstorm threaten to blow me headlong into the darkest depths. Have such hateful words ever come from the mouth of a human being before? Have such damnable words ever reached the ears of a human being before? Have such – (An explosion of derisive laughter.) Even the bandit went pale when he heard her. She clung to his arm and screamed again, 'Kill him!' The bandit stared at her, saying neither that he would kill me nor that he would not. The next thing I knew, however, he sent my wife sprawling on the bamboo leaves with a single kick. (Another explosion of derisive laughter.) The bandit calmly folded his arms and turned to look at me.

'What do you want me to do with her?' he asked. 'Kill her or let her go? Just nod to answer. Kill her?' For this if for nothing else, I am ready to forgive the bandit his crimes. (Second long silence.)

When I hesitated with my answer, my wife let out a scream and darted into the depths of the bamboo thicket. He sprang after her, but I don't think he even managed to lay a hand on her sleeve. I watched the spectacle as if it were some kind of vision.

After my wife ran off, the bandit picked up my sword and bow and arrows, and he cut my ropes at one place. 'Now it's my turn to run,' I remember hearing him mutter as he disappeared from the thicket. Then the whole area was quiet. No – I could hear someone weeping. While I was untying myself, I listened to the sound, until I realized – I realized that I was the one crying. (Another long silence.)

I finally raised myself, exhausted, from the foot of the tree. Lying there before me was the dagger that my wife had dropped. I picked it up and shoved it into my chest. Some kind of bloody mass rose to my mouth, but I felt no pain at all. My chest grew cold, and then everything sank into stillness. What perfect silence! In the skies above that grove on the hidden side of the mountain, not a single bird came to sing. The lonely glow of the sun lingered among the high branches of cedar and bamboo. The sun – but gradually, even that began to fade, and with it the cedars and bamboo. I lay there wrapped in a deep silence.

Then stealthy footsteps came up to me. I tried to see who it was, but the darkness had closed in all around me. Someone – that someone gently pulled the dagger from my chest with an invisible hand. Again a rush of blood filled my mouth, but then I sank once and for all into the darkness between lives.

Death Register

1

My mother was a madwoman. I never did feel close to her, as a son should feel toward his mother. Hair held in place by a comb, she would sit alone all day puffing on a long, skinny pipe in the house of my birth family in Tokyo's Shiba Ward. She had a tiny face on a tiny body, and that face of hers, for some reason, was always ashen and lifeless. Once, reading *The Story of the Western Wing*, I came upon the phrase 'smell of earth, taste of mud', and thought immediately of my mother – of her emaciated face in profile.

And so I never had the experience of a mother's care. I do seem to recall that one time, when my adoptive mother made a point of taking me upstairs to see her, she suddenly conked me on the head with her pipe. In general, though, she was a quiet lunatic. I or my elder sister would sometimes press her to paint a picture for us, and she would do it on a sheet of paper folded in four. And not just with black ink, either. She would apply my sister's watercolors to blossoming plants or the costumes of children on an outing. The people in her pictures, though, always had fox faces.

My mother died in the autumn of my eleventh year, not so much from illness, I think, as from simply wasting away. I have a fairly clear memory of the events surrounding her death.

A telegram must have arrived to alert us. Late on a windless night, I climbed into a rickshaw with my adoptive mother and sped across the city from Honjo to Shiba. Otherwise in my life I have never used a scarf, but I do recall that on that particular night I had a thin silk handkerchief wrapped around my neck. I also recall that it had some kind of Chinese landscape motif, and that it smelled strongly of Iris Bouquet.

My mother lay on a futon in the eight-mat parlor directly beneath her upstairs room. I knelt beside her, wailing, with my four-year-older sister. I felt especially miserable when I heard someone behind me say, 'The end is near.' My mother had been lying there as good as dead, but suddenly she opened her eyes and spoke. Sad as everyone felt, we couldn't help giggling.

I stayed up by my mother through the following night as well, but that night, for some reason, my tears simply wouldn't flow. Ashamed to be so unfeeling while right next to me my sister wept almost constantly, I struggled

17

to pretend. Yet I also believed that as long as I was unable to cry, my mother would not die.

On the evening of the third day, though, she did die, with very little suffering. A few times before it happened, she would seem to regain consciousness, look us all in the face, and release an endless stream of tears, but as usual she said not a thing.

Even after her body had been placed in the coffin, I couldn't keep from breaking down time and again. The old woman we called our 'Ōji Auntie', a distant relative, would say, 'I'm so impressed with you!' My only thought was that here was a person who let herself be impressed by very strange things.

The day of my mother's funeral, my sister climbed into a rickshaw holding the memorial tablet, and I followed her inside, holding the censer. I dozed off now and then, waking with a start each time the censer was about to drop from my hand. Still, we seemed never to reach Yanaka. Always I would wake to find the long funeral procession still winding its way through the streets of Tokyo in the autumn sunlight.

The anniversary of my mother's death is 28 November. The priest gave her the posthumous name of Kimyōin Myōjō Nisshin Daishi. I can remember neither the anniversary of my birth father's death two decades later nor his posthumous name. Memorizing such things had probably been a matter of pride for me at the age of eleven.

2

I have just the one elder sister. Not very healthy, she is nevertheless the mother of two children. She is not, of course, one of those I want to include in this 'Death Register.' Rather, it is the sister who died suddenly just before I was born. Among us three siblings, she was said to be the smartest.

She was certainly the first – which is why they named her 'Hatsuko' (First Daughter). Even now a small framed portrait of 'Little Hatsu' adorns the Buddhist altar in my house. There is nothing at all sickly-looking about her. Her cheeks, with their little dimples, are as round as ripe apricots.

Little Hatsu was by far the one who received the greatest outpouring of love from my parents. They made a point of sending her all the way from Shiba Shinsenza to attend the kindergarten of a Mrs Summers – I think it was – in Tsukiji. On weekends, though, she would stay with my mother's family, the Akutagawas, in Honjo. On these outings of hers, Little Hatsu would probably wear Western dresses, which still, in the Meiji twenties, would have seemed very modish. When I was in elementary school, I remember, I used to get remnants of her clothes to put on my rubber doll. Without exception, all the cloth patches were imported calico scattered with tiny printed flowers or musical instruments.

Ryūnosuke Akutagawa

One Sunday afternoon in early spring, when Little Hatsu was strolling through the garden (wearing a Western dress, as I imagine her), she called out to our aunt Fuki in the parlor, 'Auntie, what's the name of this tree?'

'Which one?'

'This one, with the buds.'

In the garden of my mother's family, a single low *boke** trailed its branches over the old well. Little Hatsu, in pigtails, was probably looking up at its thorny branches with big round eyes.

'It has the same name as you,' my aunt said, but before she could explain her joke, Hatsu made up one of her own:

'Then it must be a "dummy" tree.'

My aunt always tells this story whenever the conversation turns to Little Hatsu. Indeed, it's the only story left to tell about her. Probably not too many days later, Little Hatsu was in her coffin. I don't remember the posthumous name engraved on her tiny memorial tablet. I do have a strangely clear memory of her death date, though: 5 April.

For some unknown reason, I feel close to this sister I never knew. If 'Little Hatsu' were still living, she would

---

*   *boke*: The name of the tree, known as a Japanese quince (*Pyrus japonica*) in English, is a homonym for 'dimwit'. Before the aunt can joke with her that both she and the tree are '*boke*', Hatsu cleverly makes up her own remarkably similar word play using '*baka*' (dummy).

20

be over forty now. And maybe, at that age, she would look like my mother as I recall her upstairs in the Shiba house, blankly puffing away on her pipe. I often feel as if there is a fortyish woman somewhere – a phantom not exactly my mother nor this dead sister – watching over my life. Could this be the effect of nerves wracked by coffee and tobacco? Or might it be the work of some supernatural power giving occasional glimpses of itself to the real world?

3

Because my mother lost her mind, I was adopted into the family of her elder brother shortly after I was born, and so my real father was another parent for whom I had little feeling. He owned a dairy and seems to have been a small-scale success. That father was the person who taught me all about the newly imported fruits and drinks of the day: *banana*, *ice cream*, *pineapple*, *rum* – and probably much more. I remember once drinking rum in the shade of an oak tree outside the pasture, which was then located in Shinjuku. Rum was an amber-colored drink with little alcohol.

When I was very young, my father would try to entice me back from my adoptive family by plying me with these rare treats. I remember how he once openly tempted me into running away while feeding me ice cream in the Uoei restaurant in Ōmori. At times like this he could be a smooth talker and exude real charm. Unfortunately for him, though, his enticements never worked. This was because I loved my adoptive family too much – and especially my mother's elder sister, Aunt Fuki.

My father had a short temper and was always fighting with people. When I was in the third year of middle school, I beat him at sumo wrestling by tripping him backwards using a special judo move of mine. He got up and came right after me saying 'One more go.' I threw him easily again. He came charging at me for a third time, again saying 'One more go,' but now I could see he was angry. My other aunt (Aunt Fuyu, my mother's younger sister – by then my father's second wife) was watching all this, and she winked at me a few times behind my father's back. After grappling with him for a little while, I purposely fell over backwards. I'm sure if I hadn't lost to him, I would have ended up another victim of my father's temper.

When I was twenty-eight and still teaching, I received a telegram saying 'Father hospitalized,' and I rushed from Kamakura to Tokyo. He was in the Tokyo Hospital with influenza. I spent the next three days there with my Aunts Fuyu and Fuki, sleeping in a corner of the room. I was beginning to feel bored when a call came for me from an Irish reporter friend inviting me out for a meal at a Tsukiji tea house. Using his upcoming departure for America as an excuse, I left for Tsukiji even though my father was on the verge of death.

We had a delightful Japanese dinner in the company of four or five geisha. I think the meal ended around ten o'clock. Leaving the reporter, I was headed down the steep, narrow stairway when, from behind, I heard a soft feminine voice calling me 'Ah-san' in that playful geisha way. I stopped in mid-descent and turned to look up toward the top of the stairs. There, one of the geisha was looking down, her eyes fixed on mine. Wordlessly, I continued down the stairs and stepped into the cab waiting at the front door. The car moved off immediately, but instead of my father what came to mind was the fresh face of that geisha in her Western hairstyle – and in particular her eyes.

Back at the hospital, I found my father eagerly awaiting my return. He sent everyone else outside the two-panel folding screen by the bed, and, gripping and caressing my hand, he began to talk about long-ago matters that I had never known – things from the time when he married my mother. They were inconsequential things – how he and she had gone to shop for a storage chest, or how they had eaten home-delivered sushi – but before I knew it my eyelids were growing hot inside, and down my father's wasted cheeks, too, tears were flowing.

My father died the next morning without a great deal of suffering. His mind seemed to grow confused before he died, and he would say things like 'Here comes a warship! Look at all the flags it has flying! Three cheers, everybody!' I don't remember his funeral at all. What I do remember is that when we transported his body from the hospital to his home, a great big spring moon was shining down on the hearse.

4

In mid-March of this year, when it was still cold enough for us to carry pocket warmers, my wife and I visited the cemetery for the first time in a long while – a very long while. Still, however, there was no change at all in either the small grave itself (of course) nor in the red pine stretching its branches above it.

The bones of all three people I have included in this 'Death Register' lie buried in the same corner of the cemetery in Yanaka – indeed, beneath the same gravestone. I recalled the time my mother's coffin was gently lowered into the grave. They must have done the same with Little Hatsu. In my father's case, though, I remember the gold teeth mixed in with the tiny white shards of bone at the crematorium.

I don't much like visiting the cemetery, and I would prefer to forget about my parents and sister if I could. On that particular day, though, perhaps because I was physically debilitated, I found myself staring at the blackened gravestone in the early spring afternoon sunlight and wondering which of the three had been the most fortunate.

> A shimmering of heat –
> Outside the grave
> Alone I dwell.

Never before had I sensed these feelings of Jōsō's pressing in upon me with the force they truly had for me that day.

The Life of a Stupid Man

To my friend, Kume Masao:

I leave it to you to decide when and where to publish
this manuscript – or whether to publish it at all.

You know most of the people who appear here, but if
you do publish this, I don't want you adding an index
identifying them.

I am living now in the unhappiest happiness imaginable.
Yet, strangely, I have no regrets. I just feel sorry for anyone
unfortunate enough to have had a bad husband, a bad son,
a bad father like me. So goodbye, then. I have not tried –
consciously, at least – to vindicate myself here.

Finally, I entrust this manuscript to you because I believe
you probably know me better than anyone else. I may wear
the skin of an urbane sophisticate, but in this manuscript
I invite you to strip it off and laugh at my stupidity.

Akutagawa Ryūnosuke

20 June 1927

1. THE ERA

He was upstairs in a bookstore. Twenty years old at the time, he had climbed a ladder set against a bookcase and was searching for the newly-arrived Western books: Maupassant, Baudelaire, Strindberg, Ibsen, Shaw, Tolstoy . . .

The sun threatened to set before long, but he went on reading book spines with undiminished intensity. Lined up before him was not so much an array of books as the *fin de siècle* itself. Nietzsche, Verlaine, the Goncourt brothers, Dostoevsky, Hauptmann, Flaubert . . .

He took stock of their names as he struggled with the impending gloom. The books began to sink into the somber shadows. Finally his stamina gave out and he made ready to climb down. At that very moment, directly overhead, a single bare light bulb came on. Standing on his perch on top of the ladder, he looked down at the clerks and customers moving among the books. They were strangely small – and shabby.

Life is not worth a single line of Baudelaire.

He stood on the ladder, watching them below . . .

2. MOTHER

All the lunatics had been dressed in the same gray clothing, which seemed to give the large room an even more depressing look. One of them sat at an organ, playing a hymn over and over with great intensity. Another was dancing – or, rather, leaping about – in the very center of the room.

He stood watching this spectacle with a doctor of notably healthy complexion. Ten years earlier, his mother had been in no way different from these lunatics. In no way. And in fact in their smell he caught a whiff of his own mother's smell.

'Shall we go, then?'

The doctor led him down a corridor to another room. In a corner there were several brains soaking in large jars of alcohol. On one of the brains he noticed something faintly white, almost like a dollop of egg white. As he stood there chatting with the doctor, he thought again of his mother.

'The man who had this brain here was an engineer for the XX lighting company. He always thought of himself as a big shiny black dynamo.'

To avoid the doctor's eyes, he kept looking out the window. There was nothing out there but a brick wall topped with embedded broken bottles. It did, though, have thin growths of moss in dull white patches.

3. THE HOUSE

He was living in the upstairs room of a house in the suburbs. The second story tilted oddly because the ground was unstable.

In this room, his aunt would often quarrel with him, though not without occasional interventions from his adoptive parents. Still, he loved this aunt more than anyone. She never married, and by the time he was twenty, she was an old woman close to sixty.

He often wondered, in that suburban second story, if people who loved each other had to cause each other pain. Even as the thought crossed his mind, he was aware of the floor's eerie tilt.

4. TOKYO

A thick layer of cloud hung above the Sumida River. From the window of the little steamer, he watched the Mukōjima bank drawing closer. To his eyes, the blossoming cherry trees there looked as dreary as rags in a row. But almost before he knew it, in those trees – those cherry trees that had lined the bank of Mukōjima since the Edo Period – he was beginning to discover himself.

5. EGO

He and an elder colleague sat at a café table puffing on cigarettes. He said very little, but he paid close attention to his companion's every word.

'I spent half the day riding around in an automobile.'

'Was there something you needed to do?'

Cheek resting on his hand, the elder colleague replied with complete abandon, 'No, I just felt like riding around.'

The words released him into a world of which he knew nothing – a world of 'ego' close to the gods. He felt a kind of pain but, at the same time, a kind of joy.

The café was extremely small. Beneath a framed picture of the god Pan, however, a rubber tree in a red pot thrust its thick leaves out and down.

6. ILLNESS

In a steady ocean breeze, he spread out the large English dictionary and let his fingertip find words for him.

Talaria: A winged sandal.

Tale: A story.

Talipot: A coconut palm native to the East Indies. Trunk from 50 to 100 feet in height, leaves used for umbrellas, fans, hats, etc. Blooms once in 70 years . . .

His imagination painted a vivid picture of this bloom.

He then experienced an unfamiliar scratchy feeling in his throat, and before he knew it he had dropped a glob of phlegm on the dictionary. Phlegm? But it was not phlegm. He thought of the shortness of life and once again imagined the coconut blossom – the blossom of the coconut palm soaring on high far across the ocean.

7. PICTURE

It happened for him suddenly – quite suddenly. He was standing outside a bookstore, looking at a Van Gogh volume, when he suddenly understood what a 'picture' was. True, the Van Gogh was just a book of reproductions, but even in the photographs of those paintings, he sensed the vivid presence of nature.

This passion for pictures gave him a whole new way of looking at the world. He began to pay constant attention to the curve of a branch or the swell of a woman's cheek.

One rainy autumn evening, he was walking beneath an iron railroad bridge in the suburbs. Below the bank on the far side of the bridge stood a horse cart. As he passed it, he sensed that someone had come this way before. Someone? There was no need for him to wonder who that 'someone' might have been. In his twenty-three-year-old heart, a Dutchman with a cut ear and a long pipe in his mouth was fixing his gaze on this dreary landscape.

8. SPARKS: FLOWERS OF FIRE

Soaked by the rain, he trod along the asphalt. It was a heavy downpour. In the enveloping spray, he caught the smell of his rubberized coat.

Just then he saw the overhead trolley line giving off purple sparks and was strangely moved. His jacket pocket concealed the manuscript of the piece he was planning to publish in their little magazine. Walking through the rain, he looked back and up once again at the trolley line.

The cable was still sending sharp sparks into the air. He could think of nothing in life that he especially desired, but those purple sparks – those wildly-blooming flowers of fire – he would trade his life for the chance to hold them in his hands.

9. CADAVERS

A tag on a wire dangled from the big toe of each cadaver. The tags were inscribed with names, ages, and such. His friend bent over one corpse, peeling back the skin of its face with a deftly wielded scalpel. An expanse of beautiful yellow fat lay beneath the skin.

He studied the cadaver. He needed to do this to finish writing a story – a piece set against a Heian Period background – but he hated the stink of the corpses, which was like the smell of rotting apricots. Meanwhile, with wrinkled brow, his friend went on working his scalpel.

'You know, we're running out of cadavers these days,' his friend said.

His reply was ready: 'If *I* needed a corpse, I'd kill someone without the slightest malice.' Of course the reply stayed where it was – inside his heart.

10. THE MASTER

He was reading the Master's book beneath a great oak tree. Not a leaf stirred on the oak in the autumn sunlight. Far off in the sky, a scale with glass pans hung in perfect balance. He imagined such a vision as he read the Master's book . . .

11. DAWN

Night gradually gave way to dawn. He found himself on a street corner surveying a vast market. The swarming people and vehicles in the market were increasingly bathed in rose light.

He lit a cigarette and ambled into the market. Just then a lean black dog started barking at him, but he was not afraid. Indeed, he even loved this dog.

In the very center of the marketplace, a sycamore spread

its branches in all directions. He stood at the foot of the tree and looked up through the branches at the sky. A single star shone directly above him.

It was his twenty-fifth year – the third month after he first met the Master.

12. NAVAL PORT

Gloom filled the interior of the miniature submarine. Crouching down amid all the machinery, he peered into a small scope. What he saw there was a view of the bright naval port.

'You should be able to see the *Kongō*, too,' the naval officer explained to him.

As he was looking at the small warship through the square eyepiece, the thought of parsley popped into his mind for no reason – faintly aromatic parsley on top of a thirty-yen serving of beefsteak.

13. THE MASTER'S DEATH

In the wind after the rain, he walked down the platform of the new station. The sky was still dark. Across from the platform three or four railway laborers were swinging picks and singing loudly. The wind tore at the men's song and at his own emotions.

He left his cigarette unlit and felt a pain close to joy. 'Master near death,' read the telegram he had thrust into his coat pocket.

Just then the 6 a.m. Tokyo-bound train began to snake its way toward the station, rounding a pine-covered hill in the distance and trailing a wisp of smoke.

14. MARRIAGE

The day after he married her, he delivered a scolding to his wife: 'No sooner do you arrive here than you start wasting our money.' But the scolding was less from him than from his aunt, who had ordered him to deliver it. His wife apologized to him, of course, and to the aunt as well – with the potted jonquils she had bought for him in the room.

15. HE AND SHE

They led a peaceful life, surrounded by the garden's broad green *bashō* leaves.

It helped that their house was located in a town by the shore a full hour's train ride from Tokyo.

16. PILLOW

Pillowing his head on his rose-scented skepticism, he read a book by Anatole France. That even such a pillow might hold a god half-horse, he remained unaware.

17. BUTTERFLY

A butterfly fluttered its wings in a wind thick with the smell of seaweed. His dry lips felt the touch of the butterfly for the briefest instant, yet the wisp of wing dust still shone on his lips years later.

18. MOON

He happened to pass her on the stairway of a certain hotel. Her face seemed to be bathed in moonglow even now, in daylight. As he watched her walk on (they had never met), he felt a loneliness he had not known before.

19. MAN-MADE WINGS

He moved on from Anatole France to the eighteenth-century philosophers, though not to Rousseau. Perhaps this was because one side of him – the side easily moved by passion – was too close to Rousseau. Instead, he approached the author of *Candide*, who was closer to another side of him – the cool and richly intellectual side.

At twenty-nine, life no longer held any brightness for him, but Voltaire supplied him with man-made wings.

Spreading these man-made wings, he soared with ease into the sky. The higher he flew, the farther below him sank the joys and sorrows of a life bathed in the light of intellect. Dropping ironies and smiles upon the shabby towns below, he climbed through the open sky, straight for the sun – as if he had forgotten about that ancient Greek who plunged to his death in the ocean when his man-made wings were singed by the sun.

20. SHACKLES

He and his wife came to live with his adoptive parents when he went to work for a newspaper. He saw his contract, written on a single sheet of yellow paper, as a great source of strength. Later, however, he came to realize that the contract saddled *him* with all the obligations and the company with none.

21. CRAZY GIRL

Two rickshaws sped down a deserted country road beneath overcast skies. From the sea breeze it was clear that the road was headed toward the ocean. Puzzled that he felt not the slightest excitement about this rendezvous, he sat in the second rickshaw thinking about what had drawn him here. It was certainly not love. And if it was not love, then . . . but to avoid the conclusion, he had to tell himself, *At least we are in this as equals.*

The person riding in the front rickshaw was a crazy girl. And she was not alone in her madness: her younger sister had killed herself out of jealousy.

There's nothing I can do about this anymore.

He now felt a kind of loathing for this crazy girl – this woman who was all powerful animal instinct.

The two rickshaws soon passed a cemetery where the smell of the shore was strong. Several blackened, pagoda-shaped gravestones stood within the fence, which was woven of brushwood and decorated with oyster shells. He caught a glimpse of the ocean gleaming beyond the gravestones and suddenly – inexplicably – he felt contempt for the woman's husband for having failed to capture her heart.

22. A PAINTER

It was just a magazine illustration, but the ink drawing of a rooster showed a remarkable individuality. He asked a friend to tell him about the painter.

A week later, the painter himself came to pay him a visit. This was one of the most remarkable events in his entire life. He discovered in this painter a poetry of which no one else was aware. In addition, he discovered in himself a soul of which he himself had been unaware.

One chilly autumn evening, he was reminded of the painter by a stalk of corn: the way it stood there armed in its rough coat of leaves, exposing its delicate roots atop the mounded earth like so many nerves, it was also a portrait of his own most vulnerable self. The discovery only served to increase his melancholy.

It's too late now. But when the time comes . . .

23. THE WOMAN

From where he stood, the plaza was beginning to darken. He walked into the open space feeling slightly feverish. The electric lights in the windows of several large office buildings flashed against the clear, faintly silvery sky.

He halted at the curb and decided to wait for the woman there. Five minutes later she came walking toward him looking somewhat haggard. 'I'm exhausted,' she said with a smile when she caught sight of him. They walked through the fading light of the plaza side-by-side. This was their first time together. He felt ready to abandon anything and everything to be with her.

In the automobile she stared at him and asked, 'You're not going to regret this?'

'Not at all,' he answered with conviction.

She pressed her hand on his and said, 'I know *I* won't have any regrets.'

Again, as she said this, her face seemed to be bathed in moonlight.

24. THE BIRTH

He stood by the sliding screen, looking down at the midwife in her white surgical gown washing the baby. Whenever soap got in its eyes, the baby would wrinkle up its sad little face and let out a loud wail. It looked like a baby rat, and its odor stirred him to these irrepressible thoughts –

Why did this one have to be born – to come into the world like all the others, this world so full of suffering? Why did this one have to bear the destiny of having a father like me?

This was the first son his wife bore him.

25. STRINDBERG

He stood in the doorway, watching some grimy Chinese men playing Mahjongg in the moonlight where figs bloomed. Back in his room, he started reading *The Confessions of a Fool* beneath a squat lamp. He had barely read two pages when he caught himself with a sour smile. So – the lies that Strindberg wrote to his lover, the Countess, were hardly different from his own.

26. ANTIQUITY

He was nearly overwhelmed by peeling Buddhas, heavenly beings, horses and lotus blossoms. Looking up at them, he forgot everything – even his good fortune at having escaped the clutches of the crazy girl.

27. SPARTAN DISCIPLINE

He was walking down a back street with a friend when a hooded rickshaw came charging in their direction. He was surprised to recognize the passenger as the woman he had been with the night before. Her face seemed to be bathed in moonglow even now, in the daylight. With his friend present, they could not exchange even ordinary greetings.

'Pretty woman,' his friend said.

Eyes on the spring hills at the end of the street, he answered without the slightest hesitation:

'Yes, very.'

28. MURDER

The country road stank of cow manure in the sun. Mopping his sweat, he struggled up the steep hill. The ripened wheat on either side of the road gave off a pleasant scent.

'Kill him, kill him . . .'

Before he knew it, he was muttering this aloud to himself over and over. Kill whom? It was obvious to him. He recalled the cringing fellow with close-cropped hair.

Just then, the domed roof of a Catholic church appeared beyond the yellow wheat.

29. FORM

It was a cast-iron saké bottle. With its finely incised lines, it had managed at some point to teach him the beauty of 'form'.

30. RAIN

In the big bed he talked with her about many things. Beyond the bedroom window it was raining. The blossoms of the crinum tree had begun to rot in the rain, it seemed. Her face, as always, looked as if it were in moonlight, yet talking with her was not entirely free of boredom. He lay on his stomach, had himself a quiet smoke, and realized he had now been with her for seven years.

Do I still love this woman? he asked himself. He was in the habit of observing himself so closely that the answer came as a surprise to him: *I do.*

31. THE GREAT EARTHQUAKE

The odor was something close to overripe apricots. Catching a hint of it as he walked through the charred ruins, he found himself thinking such thoughts as these: *The smell of corpses rotting in the sun is not as bad as I would have expected.* When he stood before a pond where bodies were piled upon bodies, however, he discovered that the old Chinese expression, 'burning the nose', was no mere sensory exaggeration of grief and horror. What especially moved him was the corpse of a child of twelve or thirteen. He felt something like envy as he looked at it, recalling such expressions as 'Those whom the gods love die young.' Both his sister and his half-brother had lost their houses to fire. His sister's husband, though, was on a suspended sentence for perjury.

Too bad we didn't all die.

Standing in the charred ruins, he could hardly keep from feeling this way.

32. FIGHT

He had a quarrel with his half-brother that ended in a physical brawl. True, he was a constant source of pressure for this younger brother, who in turn cost him a good deal of freedom. Relatives were always telling the young man, 'be like your brother', but for him, this was like being bound hand and foot. Locked in each other's grip, they fell near the edge of the veranda. He still remembers the one crape myrtle bush in the garden by the veranda – its load of brilliant red blossoms beneath a sky about to drop its rainy burden.

33. HERO

From the window of Voltaire's house, he found himself looking up toward a high mountain. There was nothing to be seen on the glacier-topped mountain, not even a vulture. There was, however, a short Russian man doggedly climbing the trail.

After night fell, beneath the bright lamp in Voltaire's house, he wrote this didactic poem (still picturing that Russian man climbing the mountain).

> You who more than anyone obeyed the Ten
>   Commandments
> Are you who more than anyone broke the Ten
>   Commandments.
>
> You who more than anyone loved the masses
> Are you who more than anyone despised the masses.
>
> You who more than anyone burned with ideals
> Are you who more than anyone knew reality.
>
> You are what our Eastern world has bred –
> An electric locomotive that smells of flowering
>   grasses.

34. COLOR

At thirty he found himself loving a piece of vacant land. It contained only some moss and scattered bits of brick and tile. To his eyes, however, it was exactly like a Cezanne landscape.

He suddenly recalled his passions of seven or eight years earlier. And when he did so, he realized that seven or eight years earlier he had known nothing about color.

35. COMIC PUPPET

He wanted to live life so intensely that he could die at any moment without regrets. But still, out of deference to his adoptive parents and his aunt, he kept himself in check. This created both light and dark sides to his life. Seeing a comic puppet in a Western tailor's shop made him wonder how close he himself was to such a figure. His self beyond consciousness, however – his 'second self' – had long since put such feelings into a story.

36. TEDIUM

He was walking through a field of plume grass with a university student. 'You fellows still have a strong will to live, I suppose?'

'Yes, of course, but you, too . . .'

'Not any more,' he said. He was telling the truth. At some point he had lost interest in life. 'I *do* have the will to create, though.'

'But surely the will to create is a form of the will to live . . . ?'

To this he did not reply. Above the field's red plumes rose the sharp outline of an active volcano. He viewed the peak with something close to envy, though he had no idea why this was so . . .

37. 'WOMAN OF HOKURIKU'

He met a woman he could grapple with intellectually. He barely extricated himself from the crisis by writing a number of lyric poems, some under the title 'Woman of Hokuriku'. These conveyed a sense of heartbreak as when one knocks away a brilliant coating of snow frozen onto a tree trunk.

> Hat of sedge dancing in the wind:
> How could it fail to drop into the road?
> What need I fear for my name?
> For your name alone do I fear.

38. PUNISHMENT

They were on the balcony of a hotel surrounded by trees in bud. He was drawing pictures to amuse a little boy – the only son of the crazy girl, with whom he had broken off relations seven years earlier.

The crazy girl lit a cigarette and watched them play. With an oppressive feeling, he went on drawing trains and airplanes. Fortunately, the boy was not his, but it still pained him greatly when the child called him 'uncle'.

After the boy wandered off, the crazy girl, still smoking her cigarette, said suggestively:

'Don't you think he looks like you?'

'Not at all. Besides –'

'But you do know about "prenatal influence", I'm sure.'

He looked away from her in silence, but in his heart he wanted to strangle her.

39. MIRRORS

He was in the corner of a café, chatting with a friend. The friend was eating a baked apple and talking about the recent cold weather when he himself began to sense a certain contradiction in the conversation.

'Hey, wait a minute – you're still a bachelor, right?'

'Not exactly: I'm getting married next month.'

That silenced him. The mirrors set in the café walls reflected him in endless numbers. Coldly. Menacingly.

40. DIALOGUE

Why do you attack the present social system?

Because I see the evils that capitalism has engendered.

Evils? I thought you recognized no difference between good and evil. How do you make a living, then?

He engaged thus in dialogue with an angel – an angel in an impeccable top hat.

41. ILLNESS

He suffered an onslaught of insomnia. His physical strength began to fade as well. The doctors gave him various diagnoses – gastric hyperacidity, gastric atony, dry pleurisy, neurasthenia, chronic conjunctivitis, brain fatigue . . .

But he knew well enough what was wrong with him: he was ashamed of himself and afraid of *them* – afraid of the society he so despised.

One afternoon when snow clouds hung over the city, he was in the corner of a café, smoking a cigar and listening to music from the gramophone on the other side of the room. He found the music permeating his emotions in a strange new way. When it ended, he walked over to the gramophone to read the label on the record.

'Magic Flute – Mozart.'

All at once it became clear to him: Mozart too had broken the Ten Commandments and suffered. Probably not the way *he* had, but . . .

He bowed his head and returned to his table in silence.

42. THE LAUGHTER OF THE GODS

At thirty-five, he was walking through a pinewood with the spring sun beating down on it. He was recalling, too, the words he had written a few years earlier: 'It is unfortunate for the gods that, unlike us, they cannot commit suicide.'

43. NIGHT

Night closed in again. The rough sea sent up spray in the fading light. Beneath these skies, he married his wife anew. This brought them joy, but there was suffering as well. With them, their three sons watched the lightning over the open sea. His wife, holding one of the boys in her arms, seemed to be fighting back tears.

'See the boat over there?' he asked her.

'Yes . . .'

'That boat with the mast cracked in two . . .'

44. DEATH

Taking advantage of his sleeping alone, he tried to hang himself with a sash tied over the window lattice. When he slipped his head into the sash, however, he suddenly became afraid of death. Not that he feared the suffering he would have to experience at the moment of dying. He decided to try it again, using his pocket watch to see how long it would take. This time, everything began to cloud over after a short interval of pain. He was sure that once he got past that, he would enter death. Checking the hands of his watch, he discovered that the pain lasted one minute and twenty-some seconds. It was pitch dark outside the lattices, but the wild clucking of chickens echoed in the darkness.

45. DIVAN

Divan was giving him new inner power. This was an 'Oriental Goethe' he had not known before. He saw the author standing with quiet confidence on the Other Shore, far beyond good and evil, and he felt an envy close to despair. In his eyes, the poet Goethe was even greater than the poet Christ. For in the heart of the poet Goethe, there bloomed not only the roses of the Acropolis and Golgotha but the rose of Arabia as well. If only he had the least ability to follow in this poet's footsteps!

Once he had finished reading *Divan* and recovered somewhat from its terrifying emotional impact, he could only despise himself for having been born such a eunuch in life!

46. LIES

He felt the suicide of his sister's husband as a terrible blow. Now he was responsible for his sister's family as well. To him at least, his future looked as gloomy as the end of the day. He felt something like a sneer for his own spiritual bankruptcy (he was aware of all of his faults and weak points, every single one of them), but he went on reading one book after another. Even Rousseau's *Confessions*, though, was full of the most heroic lies. And when it came to Tōson's *New Life*, he felt he had never met such a cunning hypocrite as that novel's protagonist. The one who truly moved him, though, was François Villon. He found in that poet's many works the 'beautiful male'.

Sometimes in his dreams the image would come to him of Villon waiting to be hanged. Like Villon, he had several times nearly fallen to the ultimate depths of life, but neither his situation nor his physical energy would permit him to keep this up. He grew gradually weaker, like the tree Swift saw so long ago, withering from the top down.

47. PLAYING WITH FIRE

She had a radiant face, like the morning sun on a thin sheet of ice. He was fond of her, but he did not love her, nor had he ever laid a finger on her.

'I've heard you want to die,' she said.

'Yes – or rather, it's not so much that I want to die as that I'm tired of living.'

This dialogue led to a vow to die together.

'It would be a Platonic suicide, I suppose,' she said.

'A Platonic double suicide.'

He was amazed at his own sangfroid.

48. DEATH

He did not die with her, but he took a certain satisfaction in his never having touched her. She often spoke with him as though their dialogue had never happened. She did once give him a bottle of cyanide with the remark, 'As long as we have this, it will give us both strength.'

And it did indeed give him strength. Sitting in a rattan chair, observing the new growth of a *shii* tree, he often thought of the peace that death would give him.

49. STUFFED SWAN

With the last of his strength, he tried to write his auto-biography, but it did not come together as easily as he had hoped. This was because of his remaining pride and skepticism, and a calculation of what was in his own best interest. He couldn't help despising these qualities in himself; but neither could he help feeling that 'Everyone is the same under the skin.' He tended to think that Goethe's title 'Poetry and Truth' could serve for anyone's autobiography, but he knew that not everyone is moved by literature. His own works were unlikely to appeal to people who were not like him and had not lived a life like his – this was another feeling that worked upon him. And so he decided to write his own brief 'Poetry and Truth'.

Once he had finished writing 'The Life of a Stupid Man', he happened to see a stuffed swan in a secondhand shop. It stood with its head held high, but its wings were yellowed and moth-eaten. As he thought about his life, he felt both tears and mockery welling up inside him. All that lay before him was madness or suicide. He walked down the darkening street alone, determined now to wait for the destiny that would come to annihilate him.

50. CAPTIVE

One of his friends went mad. He had always felt close to this man because he understood far more deeply than anyone else the loneliness that lurked beneath his jaunty mask. He visited him a few times after the madness struck.

'You and I are both possessed by a demon,' the friend whispered, 'the demon of the *fin de siècle*.'

Two or three days later, he heard, the man ate roses on the way to a hot-spring resort. When the friend was hospitalized, he recalled once sending him a terra cotta piece. It was a bust of the author of *The Inspector General*, one of the friend's favorite writers. Thinking how Gogol, too, had gone mad, he could not help feeling that there was a force governing all of them.

Just as he reached the point of utter exhaustion, he happened to read Raymond Radiguet's dying words, 'God's soldiers are coming to get me,' and sensed once again the laughter of the gods. He tried to fight against his own superstitions and sentimentalism, but he was physically incapable of putting up any kind of struggle. The 'demon of the *fin de siècle*' was preying on him without a doubt. He envied medieval men's ability to find strength in God. But for him, believing in God – in God's love – was an impossibility, though even Cocteau had done it!

51. DEFEAT

The hand with the pen began to tremble, and before long he was even drooling. The only time his head ever cleared was after a sleep induced by eight-tenths of a gram of Veronal, and even then it never lasted more than thirty minutes or an hour. He barely made it through each day in the gloom, leaning as it were upon a chipped and narrow sword.